"I couldn't believe what was behind that fence. An abandoned amusement park turned private skatepark . . . it was almost too good to be true. Then it turned out that it was, in fact, too good to be true."

JASON HART

Age: 13
Hometown: Just outside Vegas

STONE ARCH BOOKS
presents

written by
MICHAEL A. STEELE

images by
FERNANDO CANO and LAURA RIVERA

a
CAPSTONE
production

Published by Stone Arch Books
A Capstone Imprint
1710 Roe Crest Drive, North Mankato, Minnesota 56003
www.capstonepub.com

Library of Congress Cataloging-in-Publication Data is
available on the Library of Congress website.
Hardcover: 978-1-4342-3845-0
Paperback: 978-1-4342-6560-9

Summary: Jason skates at an abandoned amusement park.
But plans to repair it will put an end to the ride.

Designer: Bob Lentz
Creative Director: Heather Kindseth

Design Elements: Shutterstock.

Printed in Canada.
092013   007763FRSNS14

CHAPTERS

DESERT GRIND

The morning sun washed over Desert Grind Skatepark. The spring breeze warmed the air as it seemed to blow in more and more skaters. Jason Hart found he had to wait longer and longer for a turn at a skate run. The place was filling fast.

Jason stood at the edge of one of the park's two large bowls. He tucked his shaggy hair under his helmet as he waited for the skater below. When it was finally Jason's turn, he placed the tail of his board on the lip. He hopped onto the deck and rolled in.

From what he'd heard, the park was fairly new. He could tell that was true by how easily his wheels spun on the

cement. He cut up the opposite side of the bowl and grinded across the lip. After the simple trick, he aimed his board straight down the bowl to gain speed. When he hit the other side, Jason shot over the edge and spun a 360. He got big air, spinning completely around before reentering the bowl with his trailing foot. He spun his body to face the new direction.

On the other lip, Jason didn't catch as much air. While airborne, he pulled a 180 with a nosegrab. He let go of his skateboard's nose just before his front trucks hit the bowl. With all the waiting skaters, he wanted to get off just one more trick. He rode to the top of the bowl, reversed his body, and sped straight down. When he hurtled up the other side, he had enough speed to catch some big air. Jason hit the edge and performed a 360 cannonball. While spinning in midair, he grabbed his board's nose with one hand and tail with the other. After he stuck the landing, the surrounding skaters slapped their boards against the ground in applause.

Jason moved to the plaza area. There were plenty of steps, handrails, grind boxes, and quarterpipes. Unfortunately, there were plenty of skaters, too. Jason had moved to the Las Vegas suburb just as schools were letting out for the year. It seemed that everyone had taken advantage of the summer vacation to check out the new park.

As Jason pushed toward a nearby grind box, he had to dodge several skaters zipping through the plaza. He missed all but one.

"Look out!" shouted a voice to his left.

Jason was slammed by a kid wearing every kind of safety gear imaginable. Both skaters tumbled across the hard cement.

Luckily, Jason knew how to fall to get the least amount of road rash possible. And luckily for the other kid, his pads and helmet seemed to absorb most of the shock.

"Sorry, sorry," the kid apologized. "I couldn't turn in time."

"That's okay," Jason said as he climbed to his feet. He picked up his board and helped the other kid stand up.

The kid pushed his helmet back on his head. A sprig of auburn hair jutted out. He looked about twelve, just a year younger than Jason.

"Thanks," said the kid. He jutted out a gloved hand. "I'm Ian."

Jason shook the kid's hand. "Jason." He reached down and picked up Ian's skateboard.

"Thanks," said Ian. "I'm obviously new to this."

Jason checked the board's wheels. "These trucks are way tight."

Ian pushed back his drooping helmet. "Is that bad?"

"Sometimes," Jason replied. He dug in his shorts pocket for his truck key. "You can turn better if your trucks are looser." He began making adjustments. "It might seem hard at first, but this will help build your ankle strength and balance, too."

"Hey, thanks," said Ian. "Do you skate here a lot?"

Jason finished loosening the trucks. "This is my first time." He glanced up to see even more skaters had arrived. "And probably my last. It's way too crowded."

"Yeah, I guess so," said Ian.

"Try it now," said Jason. He handed the board back to Ian.

Ian hopped on and gave it a push. He wobbled and almost wiped out on the spot. Jason grabbed his arm and steadied him.

"Bend your knees more," Jason instructed. "Lower your center of gravity."

Ian did as he was told and immediately stabilized. "Hey, that's better." He pushed a few feet away and leaned into a turn. It wasn't a tight turn or even close to graceful, but he stayed atop his board. "And I can turn now. Thanks!"

"No worries," said Jason. He dropped his board and skated toward the exit.

"Hey, if you come back, can you teach me some tricks?" asked Ian.

Jason gave him a wave without looking back. "Yeah, sure," he said. But Jason was pretty sure that he wasn't coming back.

MEET THE CREW

Jason ollied over the curb and pushed up the driveway. He popped up his board and carried it up the sidewalk to the latest rental house. Walking through the front door, he set his board on a stack of unpacked boxes. Jason's room was filled with similar boxes that he was supposed to be unpacking. But he'd learned a long time ago not to get too settled. He never knew when his dad would decide it was time to move again.

"Is that you, Jason?" his father called from the kitchen.

"Yeah, Pop," replied Jason.

"Come here, son. I made you lunch."

Jason entered their small kitchen to find two place settings on the table. His father's sandwich was on his plate, half finished.

"I didn't know if you would be home for lunch," his father said as he opened the microwave. "But I made you a sandwich anyway." He pulled out a plate with a sandwich ready to go.

"Thanks," said Jason. He grabbed soda from the fridge, sat at the table, and took a bite. The sandwich was his dad's specialty — bologna with extra pickles, just the way Jason liked it.

"How is it?" his dad asked.

Jason swallowed. "All right," he replied.

Jason supposed he should be nicer to his dad, who was clearly trying to make up for the last fight. They had been bickering ever since the move.

"Hey, I have that job interview tomorrow," his dad announced. "It sounds like this could be a long one."

"That's what you said last time," snapped Jason.

"My last job *was* a long one," said his dad. "Almost a whole year."

"Yeah, and when I had finally made some friends, we moved way out here."

"Again, I'm sorry, Jason. But we have to go where the work is," his father said.

Jason sighed. "Whatever."

Suddenly Jason's sandwich didn't taste very good. He rose from the table and tossed the remainder of his sandwich into the trash. After putting his plate in the dishwasher, he grabbed an apple from the table.

Part of Jason knew he shouldn't be so hard on his dad. His father had told him several times that all his hard work was for his son. And he actually used to like moving around with his dad. His father always told him they were on a "grand adventure." Jason had liked exploring each new house, backyard, and neighborhood. Part of him still did.

But unfortunately, as Jason grew older, the adventure didn't seem so grand. He had moved away from too many friends and fun schools. Exploring new places quit making up for the fact that he found himself lonely all the time.

"You find a nice place to skate?" his dad asked, changing the subject.

"Yeah, sure," Jason replied without looking back.

He grabbed his board and headed through the front door. Throwing the board down, he hopped on and sped out of their neighborhood.

Jason pushed harder to gain speed. He ollied off the sidewalk and cut across the empty street. Then he pulled a short board slide on the opposite curb.

Jason popped onto the sidewalk and pointed his board toward a wooden retaining wall. He pushed hard off his board and ollied high into the air. He performed a 50-50, grinding across the corner of the wall on just his trucks. When he reached the end of the wall, he spun a 180 before landing back on the sidewalk.

Jason cut down a driveway and sped into the street. He checked his left for oncoming traffic. It was clear. But as he pulled into the right side of the road, he almost collided with three other skaters. Jason pulled a power slide. He turned sideways, skidding to a stop in front of the lead skater.

"Cool slide, dude," said the boy.

"Thanks," said Jason.

The lead skater stood about a foot taller than Jason. He

had long brown hair and wore a shirt with the sleeves cut off. "I'm Jesse," he said.

Jason nodded. "Jason."

Jesse jutted a thumb over his shoulder. "That's Hugo and Alex."

"What's up?" said Hugo.

Alex gave a small wave.

Hugo had short black hair and wore an oversized flannel shirt over a black T-shirt. Alex wore a trucker's cap with brown bangs almost covering his eyes. The three looked familiar, and Jesse recognized Jason too.

"Weren't you at Desert Grind earlier?" he asked.

"Yeah," said Jason. "I'm surprised you saw me. That place was way crowded."

"No kidding," Alex agreed. "That place is so weak."

"You did that 360 cannonball," said Jesse. "That was sick."

"Thanks," said Jason. "So is there a better place to skate around here?"

"Aw, yeah!" said Hugo with a wide grin.

Jesse shot Hugo a look that made the grin vanish. Then

he turned back to Jason. "So you're new to the area?" Jesse asked.

"Yeah, my dad and I just moved here," Jason said.

"Nice," said Jesse. "We can show you some good places to skate."

"Cool."

"Change of plans," Jesse told his crew. "Let's roll to that old grocery store on Frisk."

"Uh . . . all right," said Alex after he exchanged puzzled expressions with Hugo.

Jesse led the way and his crew followed. Jason brought up the rear, curious as to how cool an old grocery store would be. He was even more curious about the crew's first destination. *Where we they heading originally?*

20 QUESTIONS

The supermarket turned out to be a decent place. The store had been closed for a while, but the parking lot was still in good shape. Just a few cracks littered the surface, with the occasional weed poking through.

Jesse and his crew turned out to be good skaters. Jesse pushed away from the group to gain speed. He pulled a 360 kickflip, ollieing up and spinning his board completely around. With a flick of his toe, he flipped the board in midair. He landed flawlessly on the deck. Hugo and Alex then pulled the same trick. The 360 kickflip or tre-flip was the Holy Grail for beginning skaters. This crew had already mastered it.

Jason had done the same. So when he got a good run, he did a 360-heelflip. It was the same trick, but he flipped the board with his heel instead.

"Good one," said Hugo. He copied the move but had to plant a foot on the ground when he landed. "I almost had it."

"Try not to kick your right foot out so far," Jason said. Hugo attempted to do the trick again, and this time both feet landed on the deck. He wobbled a bit, but he made it.

"Cool, thanks," said Hugo.

The group continued to skate around the empty parking lot. They pulled flips, spins, pop shuvits, and no complies. Jesse's entire crew was pretty good. They even pulled some small jumps off the sidewalk at the front of the store. It was barely enough air for a spin or a quick nosegrab. Jason did a short nosegrind on a cement car stop. The parking lot was cool because no one bothered them or ran them off. But unfortunately, they could only pull off flat tricks.

"Any place to jump?" Jason asked.

Alex seemed about to answer but quickly closed his mouth. And there it was again — that strange look he exchanged with Hugo. Then both kids looked at Jesse.

"Sure," said Jesse. "Let's roll to the back."

The group skated around to the back of the store to the loading dock. The cement dock jutted out a few yards away from the store. Jason could see that it was long enough to get decent speed before launching off the corner.

"Looks good," said Jason when he saw it.

Alex was the first to climb the steps. He backed against the door and then ran across the dock. Halfway across, he threw down his board and hopped on. He popped off the edge and brought his board up for a smooth nosegrab.

Jesse sailed off the dock with a tre-flip — perfect landing. Hugo did a Japan air, holding the nose with one hand and spreading his other arm wide. When it was Jason's turn, he did a cannonball 180.

They spent the rest of the afternoon behind the store, catching what air they could off the loading dock. When not skating, they talked about the latest movies they had seen and the video games they had played. Jesse was the only one who seemed interested in Jason's life and what his father did.

"Construction?" Jesse asked. "That's cool. They're always building stuff around here."

"Yeah, he's going out to try to get a job tomorrow."

"So, I bet he has a lot of tools, huh?" asked Jesse.

"Sure," Jason replied.

"You guys build stuff together?"

"We used to." Jason rolled his board beneath one foot. "Not so much anymore."

Jason didn't know why Jesse was so curious about construction. He expected the other skater to bring up a project he was working on, but he never did. The subject was soon changed back to the latest skating video game.

Jason did another cannonball and then his own Japan air. Soon, everyone decided to call it a day. Before leaving, Jesse pulled Jason aside.

"Meet us here tomorrow, and we'll show you a better place to skate," whispered Jesse.

"Oh, yeah?" asked Jason.

"Yeah," Jesse replied. "Best you've ever seen."

THE BIG SECRET

The next morning, Jason woke up to the sweet smell of maple bacon. He trudged into the kitchen to find his dad had cooked bacon and scrambled eggs for breakfast. Already eating, his father smiled when Jason entered.

"Morning, son," said his dad.

Still sleepy, Jason grunted a reply. He poured himself a glass of juice and sat in front of his prepared plate. Usually, he just ate cereal for breakfast. The hot meal was an unexpected treat.

"I thought we'd have an early victory meal," his father explained, as if reading Jason's mind. "My interview is today."

Jason had forgotten. Then he noticed that his dad wore a short-sleeved button-down shirt and tie. "Oh, yeah," he mumbled through a mouthful of eggs. "Good luck."

Jason's father had often celebrated new jobs early for luck. The victory breakfast was by no means a guarantee that he'd get the job. But Jason had to admit, it worked about eighty percent of the time.

"What are your plans today?" asked his father.

"Just skating with some guys." Jason crunched on some crispy bacon.

His father's face brightened. "Ah, you found some friends?"

Jason shrugged. "Not really. Just some dudes to skate with."

"Are they nice boys?" his father asked.

Jason winced a little. "I guess so." He knew what his father meant, but it still sounded like his father thought he was six years old.

"Good to hear, son," said his dad.

Through all of their travels, Jason's father was worried about Jason hanging out with the wrong crowd. And by that, he meant kids who did drugs or vandalized property. Jason had never been drawn to those kinds of kids. It wasn't out of fear of getting caught or getting in trouble with his dad. Jason had been in trouble with his dad plenty of times. He supposed all kids had. He just found no pleasure in doing things that could potentially hurt himself or other people.

Jason didn't get the sense that Jesse and his crew were like that either. He could tell that there was something they weren't telling him. But he didn't get the feeling it was something bad. They seemed to be interested in the same kinds of things Jason was into. Skating and having fun.

Jason's father looked at his watch. "I better get going." He gulped down the last of his coffee and stood. "Wish me luck."

"Good luck, Pop," Jason said with a smile.

Jason was still upset about their latest move, but he didn't feel as mad at his dad anymore. He didn't know if it was just too early in the morning to be angry. Or maybe he was in a better mood after skating yesterday. Either way, he was glad to be rid of some of the anger. He stood and gathered the dirty dishes.

When Jason was finished, he packed his backpack with some fruit and energy drinks and headed out the door. He strapped on his helmet, threw down his board, and zipped down the driveway. Not stopping for any tricks, Jason skated down the neighborhood sidewalks toward the abandoned grocery store.

It wasn't long before he rolled into the parking lot. Jesse and his crew weren't there. Jason skated to the back but the loading dock was empty, too. He popped up his board and climbed the steps. While he waited, he did a 180 and then a switch 360 spin off the loading dock. He climbed back up and did a couple of tre-flips.

After he stuck the second landing, he skated to the front of the store. It was still empty. He wondered if Jesse and the others had punked him. Maybe they weren't as cool as he thought.

Jason skated around the empty parking lot a bit longer. Then, just as he'd made up his mind to leave, he heard the familiar sound of skateboard wheels on cement. Jesse, Alex, and Hugo appeared on the sidewalk. They cut into the parking lot and rolled toward Jason.

"Bet you thought we ditched you," said Jesse. He and Jason exchanged fist bumps.

"Just about," admitted Jason.

"It's all Hugo's fault," said Alex.

Hugo shrugged his shoulders. "Yeah," he admitted.

"Get back here, Hugo," Jesse said in a shrill voice. "You didn't take the trash down to the curb." Everyone laughed at Jesse's impression of what must have been Hugo's mom.

Hugo rolled his eyes. "I know, I know. Let's just go already."

"You ready to check out the coolest place to skate ever?" Jesse asked Jason.

"Always," Jason replied.

"All right then." He hopped on his board and pushed toward the street. "Let's go."

Jason followed the skaters as they left the parking lot and pulled onto the sidewalk. They led him back in the general direction of his house. But then they turned down the side street where he had almost crashed into them. They were traveling in the direction they had been heading when Jason first met them.

They ollied some curbs and pulled pop shuvits along the way. But everyone passed bigger obstacles without stopping to do tricks. They were a crew on a mission.

They ended up in an industrial part of town that seemed mostly abandoned. Jesse ollied off the sidewalk and into the small parking lot of an abandoned building. At first, Jason thought Jesse and his crew were heading to the warehouse itself. But at the last minute, he cut left and sped around the corner of the building. Alex and Hugo pushed to catch up.

A little hesitant, Jason slowed a bit. He didn't feel right about breaking into a warehouse, if that's what Jesse and the others had planned. He was relieved when he turned the corner and saw Hugo scramble through a small gap in a tall metal fence. A corner of the metal panel had been pulled up to create an opening just big enough to crawl through. By the time Jason reached the fence, Hugo had scrambled through.

"Come on," Jesse said from the other side.

Jason hopped off his board and pulled off his bag. He crouched and shoved them through the hole. Then he got to his knees and shimmied through the gap. Once through, he looked up, finding himself face-to-face with a snarling tiger.

DREAM PARK

"Whoa!" shouted Jason.

He scrambled back, trying to escape the tiger's jagged white teeth and outstretched claws. Unfortunately, he missed the gap and backed into the metal wall. He was trapped with the beast.

Laughter erupted around him. He looked to see Jesse and the others cutting up. Jason looked back at the tiger. It was only a life-sized statue of a tiger. An ornate pole ran straight through its back as if it were a bug in a giant insect collection. Behind the pole, a simple saddle was carved into the cat's back. It took a moment for Jason to make sense of what he was seeing. Then it hit him. The tiger had been part of huge carousel.

Jason climbed to his feet and dusted off his pants. "Very funny."

"Sorry, man," Jesse said. "Consider it an initiation." He jutted a thumb over his shoulder. "Putting the tiger there was Hugo's idea."

"You should've seen Alex when he first saw it," Hugo said. "He made it out the hole and was about to run all the way home."

"No, I wasn't," said Alex, no longer laughing.

"Then how come you were already a block away when you answered your phone?" asked Hugo.

Jason reached over and touched the tiger's nose. Then he gave it a knock. It was plastic and hollow. "Where did you get it?" he asked.

Jesse smiled. "That's the beauty of it." He spread his arms wide. "Right here."

Jason looked past the tiger and couldn't believe his eyes. Brightly colored buildings lined narrow paved streets. A tangle of roller coaster tracks twisted and looped toward the sky. An old Ferris wheel stood beside it, many of its cars missing. Jason was amazed. They stood inside of an abandoned amusement park.

"Check it," Jesse said. He hopped on his board and skated down the empty street. Jason and the others followed.

It was one of the coolest places Jason had seen. It was one thing to visit an amusement park. To have one all to yourself was a completely new experience. It was exciting and creepy at the same time.

"Cool, huh?" asked Alex.

"Uh . . . yeah," Jason replied.

They passed an old fun house. Jason watched his reflection change inside the many distorted mirrors. They passed the carousel full of detailed exotic animals (minus one tiger, of course). They passed concession stands, spinning rides, and flying rides. Most of them were faded, tangled with cobwebs, and covered with dust.

Jason skated slowly, taking it all in. He noticed that the other kids didn't simply skate through. They pulled grinds off benches and jumped off broken tables where one set of legs propped them up like ramps. They seemed to pull tricks off everything around them. Jason finally realized that they had positioned all of that stuff themselves.

"You made your own personal skatepark," Jason said.

"That's right," Hugo agreed. "*This* is the best place to skate in town."

"We didn't want to tell you at first," Jesse admitted. "We wanted to make sure you wouldn't tell all your friends."

"But since you're new in town," Alex added. "We figured you didn't have any friends."

"No offense," said Jesse.

"That's cool," Jason replied. He wasn't offended at all. In fact, he was still amazed at his surroundings.

Jason cut across the street and aimed toward a flattened corn dog sign. Its edge was propped up on the curb. He hit it fast and ollied over the edge, swinging the tail of his board around for a 180.

"Right on," said Alex.

Jason skid to a stop. "Wait a minute. Who owns this?"

Jesse shrugged. "Don't know."

"Aren't you worried about trespassing?" Jason asked. He didn't want trouble, no matter how good the skating.

"Man, no one comes here anymore," Jesse explained. "This place has been closed for years."

"Yeah, show him neon alley," said Hugo.

"Oh, yeah." Jesse waved them forward as he hopped onto his board.

After a couple more turns — littered with more homemade obstacles — they entered a street packed full of huge neon signs. The long-dead tubes were dull in color, but the metal signs on which they were attached were impressive in size and design. Stacked on end and filed between two buildings, one sign was shaped like a giant horse. There was a huge palm tree and an enormous deck of playing cards.

"So many casinos come and go, they've been parking these babies here forever," explained Jesse.

"But we haven't found any new ones in a long time," added Alex. "I think they finally forgot about this place."

At first, Jason felt uncomfortable about trespassing in the park, even though it was way cool and a once-in-a-lifetime opportunity. However, he felt a bit better knowing that it was truly abandoned. And it seemed like such a waste for no one to enjoy it.

Jesse and the others finished showing Jason around the park. There was a large dry fountain with a bowl-shaped center. It wasn't as deep as the bowls in the real skateparks, but they could catch some decent air for a spin or two.

"Show him Hugo's quarterpipe," suggested Alex.

"More like Hugo's fail pipe," chided Jesse.

Hugo waved him toward a nearby building. "No, come on. It's cool."

As they approached, Jason saw a huge metal sign with the face of a clown painted on it. The thick metal was bent in a curve and the top was attached to the building itself. Hugo kicked for more speed and then rolled up the sign. When he reached the top, he held onto a windowsill with one hand and his board with the other. He came around and rolled down the sign — a smooth backside air.

Unfortunately, when Hugo hit the bottom of the ramp, the sign detached from the building and slid away. Hugo rode it out like riding a wave.

"Fail pipe," Jesse and Alex said simultaneously.

Hugo hopped off his board. "No way, it's cool." He ran over to the sign. "You just have to reset it."

Jason could see Hugo struggling with the heavy sign so he ran to the other side to help. The two lifted the top of the flexible sign up along the wall.

"Just pin it under that nail there," Hugo instructed.

Jason saw that the sign had been wedged under a thick bent nail. After he and Hugo slid it under the bent nail on each side, Hugo pushed down on the center, making the sign curve. The bottom came to rest against two metal stakes driven into the asphalt.

"Sometimes I can get two tricks out of it," Hugo boasted.

Jason studied the ramp. "You know, some three-inch, self-tapping screws would hold that in place."

"Oh, yeah?" Hugo asked.

"Yeah," agreed Jason. "I could bring some from home and maybe my dad's impact driver."

"Man, I didn't understand half of what you just said," admitted Jesse. "But that's another reason we wanted to show you this place." He put a hand on Jason's shoulder. "With the tools and the talent, the sky's the limit."

Jason gazed around the park. His mind was filling with ideas.

The next morning, Jason's dad had already left for the day. Jason found a note scribbled on a notepad on the table.

Jason,

The victory breakfast worked. Today's my first day. Big planning meeting. I have my own team this time and the "boss" can't be late. This looks like it could be a long one!

Love,

Dad

Jason had heard this from his father many times before. His dad would estimate a job lasting years, and it would turn out to be just a few months. Unfortunately, Jason had learned the hard way to not get his hopes up.

He looked at he note again. A bright logo took up the top part of the notepad. It was a cartoon drawing of a bluebird with a red chest. There was no company name, but Jason guessed that the picture was his father's new company logo.

Jason wolfed down a bowl of cereal and headed to the garage. He moved several boxes aside until he came across the ones containing his father's tools. He rummaged through them, pulling out what he thought he could use. He grabbed the cordless impact driver and screws for Hugo's fail pipe. He also pulled out his father's large socket set and a couple of wrenches. After stowing a few other items, he zipped up his backpack. He grabbed his board and headed for the park.

The backpack felt much heavier by the time he made it to the park. He grunted as he pulled it off to shimmy through the gap in the fence. As Jason skated through the abandoned park, he realized that he was alone. He hadn't realized just how big of a hurry he'd been in to get there. He supposed his father's note had something to do with it. With his dad's promise of this being a long stay, Jason had learned to expect the opposite. Part of him wanted to enjoy as much of the old amusement park as possible before they had to move again. Still, being alone in the place seemed even creepier than before.

First stop was Hugo's quarterpipe. The ramp was still in place, so it was an easy fix. He dug out the drill and screws and set to work attaching the top to the building. The self-tapping screws drilled right through the metal and then into the wooden building on the other side. In just under five minutes, Hugo's quarterpipe was a fail pipe no more.

Jason gave it a test run. He pushed hard toward the curved sign. When he reached the top, he grabbed his board with one hand and kicked his other foot away — an almost perfect judo air. It would have been perfect if his foot hadn't brushed against the wall in midair. He didn't make the landing and ended up running after his board down the ramp.

"Okay," he said to himself. "We'll have to find a way to make a proper quarterpipe somewhere."

Jason skated around the park looking for a better quarterpipe location. Instead of finding one, he happened upon a pile of wooden benches. Most of them were broken and had been piled up for some reason. He immediately saw something he could work with. When he was finished, he hadn't built a quarterpipe, but he had made a long grind box instead. He started adding the last few screws.

"Dude," said a voice behind him.

Jason jumped and spun around. It was Jesse and his crew. With the drill going, he hadn't heard them roll up.

Hugo grinned. "This place is creepy, right?"

"You said it," Jason replied.

Jesse crouched beside the box. "Sweet grind box, man."

"Thanks," Jason added the last two screws. "You have any wax?"

"Alex." Jesse said without looking back. "Wax on, wax off, brother."

Alex dug into his pocket and pulled out a small red square of skater wax. He squatted and rubbed a hard cube along the top two corners of the box. After a couple of minutes' work, he was finished. He stood. "Who's first?"

Jesse pointed a finger at Jason. "It's your box. Go for it."

Jason pulled his tools aside and grabbed his board. He got a running start and hopped onto his board. When he neared the box, he ollied into a 5-0. His back trucks grinded along one corner of the box while the nose of his board

pointed up. It was as if he pulled a wheelie down the entire box. He ollied off at the end and skidded to a stop.

"Sick!" Jason said. "Smooth wax job, Alex."

"Nosegrind coming," called Jesse. He skated up to the box and grinded his front trucks along the edge.

"K-grind," called Hugo. He pulled a grind similar to Jesse's but with the back of the board swung out to the side.

"5-0 hand drag," called Alex. He ollied onto the box and onto his back trucks. But when he leaned back to drag his hand along the box, he lost his balance and wiped out.

"Oh!" shouted Jesse. "You got cocky!"

Jason glanced around. "Are there any stairs around?" he asked. "With handrails?"

Jesse turned to the others. "My man Jason wants to know if there are any rails around here."

Hugo raised his eyebrows. "Oh, yeah."

"Plenty," added Alex.

Jesse put a hand on Jason's shoulder and slowly spun him around. Jason looked up and saw the large wooden roller coaster looming above.

"That's right," said Jesse. "Dead rails."

BIG PLANS

Wind whipped through Jason's hair as he held tight to the rail beside him. Even though he had never been scared of heights, he felt a bit uneasy. Then again, he had never stood atop a roller coaster before.

"Quite a view, huh?" asked Jesse. The taller boy acted more confident than the others. But it didn't go unnoticed by Jason that Jesse still held tight to the rail beside him.

"Very cool," said Jason. And it was. He could see the entire park from there. He was surprised to find that there was so much more to the park than they had shown him.

"Show him the marks," said Alex.

"Oh, yeah," said Jesse. He led the way down the narrow service ramp between the rails. When they were close to the bottom of the hill, he stopped and pointed to a mark carved into the wood. "This is the highest we've ever started."

"Started what?" asked Jason.

"Our run," replied Jesse.

"*Your* run, dude," Alex clarified. "That run that almost broke your neck."

Jesse rubbed his neck. "I thought it did."

Jason looked down the rails. The bottom of the big hill dipped down and jutted back up to a smaller hill.

"You grinded down rails from here?" asked Jason.

"Well, just once," Jesse admitted.

"Man, he came down and flew off the other hill," said Hugo. "It was crazy."

"We have other marks lower down," Alex added. "If you start lower, you stop before you get to the top of that hill."

"We haven't done it in a while, though," said Hugo. "You want to try it?"

"I don't know," said Jason. It sounded cool, but it looked extremely dangerous.

"So, where did you land on your highest run?" Jason asked.

Jesse pointed to an open area just beyond the small hill. The roller coaster rails took a hard left at that point, leaving a large square inside the fence. It was covered with tall grass.

Jason squatted and looked down one of the rails. It was a smooth ride all the way down. He had to admit that he was excited about grinding down the rails. But there had to be a way to make it safer.

"He's thinking about it," Jesse said with a chuckle. "I knew he'd like this."

Jason stood and scanned the park again. "Is there a kiddie section in this place?" he asked.

"Yeah, over there." Alex pointed to the far corner of the park. "But it's pretty lame."

Jason smiled. "I have an idea."

They led him to the part of the park geared for younger kids. There were mini versions of many of the rides — little roller coasters, small Ferris wheels, and playground equipment. When they reached that section, Jason hopped off his board and went right for the playground equipment.

He scrambled over a small fence and pulled at one of the vinyl-covered pads lining the playground floor. It came up with ease.

"What are you looking for?" asked Jesse.

Jason stood and paced around the rest of the huge playground. It was a tangle of tubes, swings, and slides.

"I might have a way you can make that jump," Jason replied.

"Are you insane?" asked Hugo.

Jason didn't reply. Instead, he turned a corner and found exactly what he was looking for — the playground's old ball pit. "Check it out."

Of the three skaters, Jesse was the first to figure it out. His eyes lit. "Something to land in."

Jason grinned. "Exactly."

"So what do we do?" asked Hugo.

Jason quickly set them to work. He had Alex and Hugo gather all of the loose foam padding that wasn't rotted with age. Meanwhile, he and Jesse found some old concession carts to transport the balls. It took three trips, but they managed to move all the balls to the roller coaster.

Jason and Jesse found wooden barricades meant to direct people to different parts of the park. They were basically moveable walls. The two kids moved several of them to form a box at the bottom of the roller coaster. Once they were in place, everyone filled the box with the small plastic balls. When they were out of balls, they tore up the old foam pieces and threw them on top. The huge box brimmed with soft debris.

Hugo climbed up part of the roller coaster trestle. "Test drive!" He leaped into the box of foam. He disappeared behind the wall and bits of foam flew out. Hugo laughed. "It's great!" The rest of the boys followed his lead.

"So who's going to make the first jump?" asked Alex.

"Same as the grind box," said Jesse. "Jason's idea. He gets first shot."

Jason's heart beat faster. He was excited about trying the jump at first. But now that it was time to go through with it, he had to admit that he was a bit scared. He hated to show fear in front of his new friends.

"All right," Jason said. He tried to keep the shakiness out of his voice. "But let's do it tomorrow." It was almost sunset, and he was beat from the day's work. "I want to be at my best when I try something like that."

"That's cool," said Jesse. He seemed to understand completely. All of them did. None of them gave him any grief or called him chicken or anything. Despite the vow he made to himself about not getting close to anyone, Jason was really beginning to like these guys.

Jesse was the first to start climbing out of the box. But as soon as he was up top, he dove back in again.

"Couldn't resist one more . . ." Hugo started.

Jesse shushed him. "Someone's out there," he whispered.

Alex snickered. "Yeah, right."

"I'm serious," Jesse whispered.

Slowly, all four kids made their way to the edge and peered over the retaining walls. Sure enough, two men in white shirts walked down the nearby roadway.

"Oh, man," Jason whispered to himself.

On each man's shirt was the same logo he'd seen on his dad's note — a bluebird with a red chest.

"Are those security guards?" asked Jason.

"I don't know," replied Jesse. "This is the first time that anyone has shown up."

"Let's bounce, dude," whispered Hugo.

"Good idea," said Jason.

After the two men were out of sight, the four skaters climbed out of the foam pit. They slinked along and snatched up their boards and gear. Jason gathered his father's tools and slipped them into his backpack. He winced when two of the wrenches clinked together. Everyone froze. When they were sure that neither of the men had heard anything, Jason and the others snuck along the back wall. They slipped out through the gap in the fence and skated away from the park.

"Dude," Alex said when they were a few blocks away, "what's up with that?"

"I don't know," said Jesse. "Let's come back tomorrow and see if they're back."

"Good idea," Jason agreed.

The skaters bumped fists and went their separate ways. By the time Jason made his way home, he was beat. Between all the work they did and lugging the heavy tools back from the park, he was ready to crash. His dad's car was in the driveway, but he was nowhere to be found in the house. Jason came upon his father in the garage, digging through a large cardboard box. He also wore the same white shirt with bluebird logo that they had seen on the men in the park.

"Hey, Pop," said Jason. "What's up?"

"I can't find some of my tools," replied his dad.

"Oh," Jason shook his backpack. "I borrowed some." He unzipped his backpack and began removing them.

"Oh, yeah?" his dad said. "You have a project going?"

"Just some skate stuff," Jason replied. Before his dad

could enquire further, he added, "You never told me about your new job."

His father's face lit up. "You're going to love this." He jutted a thumb at the logo on his shirt. "This company . . . they're renovating this old amusement park at the edge of town."

Jason wasn't surprised by the answer. But his chest tightened a bit anyway.

"They have experts coming in to redesign the rides," continued his dad. "But my team is going to rebuild all the concession stands and gift shops."

Jason pretended to be excited. "Cool, Pop."

"Yeah, it's a nice long job, at least a year," his father explained. "And best of all . . . free tickets when it's open."

Big deal, Jason thought. *I get in free right now.*

DEFEND THE FORT

The next morning, Jason got out of the house as quickly as possible. Once again, his father had already gone. Jason didn't know if his father was going to the park that day or not. Either way, he wanted to warn the guys not to go in. Unfortunately, their private skatepark was no more.

Jason skated to the amusement park and waited outside the gap. Jason waited about twenty minutes. Then a thought occurred to him. What if Jesse and the others were already in the park? He didn't think it was very likely. They struck him as the type who liked to sleep in.

Jason thought he'd better be sure. He grabbed his board and crawled through. Something was wrong. He couldn't figure it out at first. Then it came to him: the tiger was missing. Had the workers taken it? It didn't seem likely since it had been placed in such a remote part of the park. That left only one answer: Jesse and his crew were already there.

Jason hopped onto his board and skated around the park. He slowed as he neared the small intersections. He didn't want to run into one of the workers or even worse, his dad.

He rolled to the front of the park and found the tiger. It now faced the main entrance. But it wasn't alone. All of the other carousel animals were there. Each plastic beast was propped up to face anyone who entered the park. Hugo and Alex pushed a large elephant to join the others.

"What are you doing?" asked Jason, skating up to them.

"Cool, huh?" asked Hugo.

"Maybe the workers will think the place is haunted and leave us alone," explained Alex.

"Dude, that's crazy," said Jason.

"You should see what Jesse has planned," said Alex. "Now *that's* crazy."

The three kids froze when a chain rattled. There was movement beyond the front turnstiles. Jason and the others

snatched up their boards and ran for the nearest building, ducking around the corner.

The boys peeked around the edge to see dozens of men and women in white shirts flood through the front gate. The animals didn't detour them. Some even used their camera phones to take pictures of themselves with the animals.

Jason couldn't see his father; they were too far away. But if Jason had to guess, his dad would be among them.

Jason pulled Alex around the corner. "Where is Jesse?"

"Neon alley," replied Alex.

Jason grabbed his board and ran down the edge of the building. When he was sure that he wouldn't be heard, he threw down his board and hopped on. Jason pushed hard, ollied over his new grind box, and then leaned hard to the left, cutting onto a side street.

Soon, Jason found himself in a power slide at the edge of neon alley. Once he had skidded to a stop, his eyes darted all around. He couldn't see Jesse anywhere.

He cupped his hands over his mouth. "Jesse?" he asked in as loud a whisper as he dared.

There was no answer. Then he spotted movement out of

the corner of his eye. He looked up and saw Jesse standing on the roof of one of the buildings lining the street.

"What are you doing?" asked Jason.

Jesse smiled. "Check it!" He extended both arms and pretended to push over one of the neon signs. "Dominoes!"

Jason knew what he meant. If one of the vertical signs fell over, it would knock into the one beside it. The chain reaction would knock all the signs over.

"I'll wait for one of them to get close," Jesse shouted.

"Someone could get hurt," Jason shouted back.

Jesse waved him off. "Nah, the signs will just hit the other building," he explained. "It'll just scare 'em."

"What if you're wrong?" asked Jason. "Dude, these signs are old. One could break in half. Glass could go everywhere."

Jesse opened his mouth to reply, then stopped. It was obvious that he hadn't thought of that scenario. Then he frowned. "Well, who cares? This is our park. They shouldn't even be here. If they get hurt, it's their fault."

"Dude," Jason pleaded. "One of *them* is my dad!"

Suddenly, Jesse ducked out of sight.

"Son?" said a voice from behind.

THE BIG BIRD

Jason, Jesse, Alex, and Hugo stood in front of twenty men and women wearing white shirts with bluebird logos. One of those people was Jason's father. Unfortunately, another one was Jason's father's boss. Jason hoped that he hadn't cost his father his job.

Jason's dad huddled in conversation with his boss and two other men.

"What are they saying?" whispered Jesse.

"I don't know," Jason replied.

"Are they going to call the cops?" asked Hugo.

Before anyone could reply, the huddle broke. The big boss led the way as the group walked toward the skaters.

"So you're Ben Hart's son," said the man. He extended a hand to Jason. "I'm James Byrd."

Jason shook the man's hand. "Hello, Mr. Byrd." Jason introduced the other skaters.

After the introductions, Mr. Byrd looked the skaters over. "I hear that you've got yourself quite the skatepark here. I'm sorry to say that we can't allow that anymore," the man continued. "But we're curious to see what you've done."

The boys led the group of men around the park, pointing out obstacles. Jesse and his crew seemed reluctant at first. But their pride soon began showing through.

"The picnic tables make great ramps and roll-ins," Jesse explained. He threw down his board and hopped on. Soon, he flew off the end of a picnic table ramp. He pulled a smooth tre-flip in the process.

Hugo pulled a 360 spin at the top of his quarterpipe. "It's way cooler since Jason fixed it."

"Show them your grind box, Jason," Alex suggested.

Jason led them over to his extra long grind box. He ollied into a 5-0 and then pulled a nosegrind halfway down. At the end of the box, he dismounted with a 180 spin.

"Very impressive, boys," said Mr. Byrd. "Is that all?"

Jason and the others looked at each other and shrugged. They might as well show him everything.

The skaters led the group to the roller coaster. Jason and Jesse pointed out the foam landing box and the marks midway up the larger hill.

"That's insane," said Mr. Byrd. "You actually jumped this?"

"I never got a chance," Jason admitted. "We just finished it yesterday."

"I don't think you're ever going to try it," said his dad. "That looks way too dangerous."

"Actually, long jump snow skiers practice on similar setups during the summer months," said one of the men.

"Is that right?" asked Mr. Byrd.

"Yes, sir," replied the man. "With the proper precautions, it's actually quite safe."

"I wonder how much something like that would cost," said Mr. Byrd. The wheels seemed to be spinning in his mind.

"Do any other amusement parks have skateparks in them?" Jason asked, hoping he already knew the answer.

"No, Jason," said Mr. Byrd with a smile. "No they don't."

ONE YEAR LATER

Jason tightened his helmet strap and checked his wrist guards, elbow pads, and kneepads. Normally, he didn't wear quite as much padding. But it was mandatory when going down the skatepark's biggest attraction — Dead Rails.

Mr. Byrd had built an amazing skatepark into his amusement park. It was loaded with bowls, halfpipes, quarterpipes, grind boxes, ramps, and rails. But the biggest and best part was the tall ramp and rail set.

Based on Jesse's and Jason's idea, a huge ramp stretched dozens of feet into the air. It wasn't what Jason had set up, but it resembled a wrecked roller coaster on purpose. Skaters could roll down the ramp or grind down either of the two rails. Once they hit the bottom, their momentum would propel them high into the air. Skaters got tons of airtime to pull off the sickest of tricks. Then they would land in a foam pit three times the size of the one Jason originally built. Skaters had to pad up from head to toe. There was also a safety harness with a thin cable attached to a remote crane above. Sometimes the cable got in the way of tricks. But with enough practice it was easy to work around.

Jason had plenty of practice since he had free admission to the park anytime he liked. There were perks to having a father who worked at the park and being one of the four main skating consultants. Jason, Jesse, Alex, and Hugo had helped Mr. Byrd's people design the skatepark.

Jason looked down at the waiting crowd below. His crew was there cheering him on.

"Rock on!" shouted Hugo.

"Pop it!" shouted Jesse.

Jason pushed down the ramp. He chose not to grind down the rails; he was going for speed. He bent his knees and leaned forward to gain even more speed. As he neared the dip, he twisted his body. By the time he hit the jump, his body was a spring. He grabbed his board with one hand and swung his other arm wide. While rocketing through the air, he spun around two complete times. It was a 720 — a very rare and difficult trick. Jason dropped into the foam pit wearing a wide grin.

Jason climbed the ladder out of the pit. He set his board down beside a bench and began removing his pads. Just then, a familiar face appeared in front of him.

"Sick trick, Jason." It was Ian Jacobs, one of the first skaters he'd met almost a year ago. When he'd met Ian, the young boy was covered in pads. Now, Ian simply wore a helmet, and Jason was the one covered in pads.

"Check it," said Ian. He gave his board a kick and pulled a 360 kickflip. The landing was sketchy, but he'd come a long way since the first day they'd met.

"Good job, dude," said Jason. "You're almost there."

"Thanks for helping me," said Ian.

Jason smiled as the younger boy skated off into the crowd. Ian was just one of many, many friends Jason had made in his new hometown.

Jason's dad was right: this job was a long one. The construction work turned into maintenance work once the amusement park opened. Jason skates the Dead Rails as often as he can. It's like a second home, which means a lot to a kid like Jason.

L2S Revive

L2S Hart Hawk Face

L2S Dead Rails

SKATE CLINIC:

Approach the ledge in an ollie stance, going a comfortable speed. The faster you go, the farther you will grind.

Ollie up onto the ledge, putting all your weight onto your back trucks. Holding your arms out to the side will help you balance.

Make sure to point the nose of the skateboard up and off to the side through the grind. Then you'll be able to drop off of the ledge at any time.

When you want to get off the ledge, drop off and ride away.

SKATE CLINIC:
TERMS

50-50 grind
a move where a skater pops up onto an obstacle, then grinds his or her back truck along it and suspends the front truck above the edge

cannonball
an aerial move where the skater grabs the nose of the board with the front hand and the tail with the back hand

heelflip
a move where the skater flips the board over with his or her heel

Japan air
a move where the skater grabs the toe edge of the skateboard with the front hand between the trucks and twists his or her body so that the board is pulled behind the skater. The free arm is flung out wide.

judo air
an aerial move where the skater grabs the skateboard near the nose and kicks the front foot off the toe side

kickflip
a move where the skater pops the skateboard into the air and flicks it with the front foot to make it flip all the way around in the air before the skater lands on the board again

no comply
a move where the skater does an ollie movement using only the back foot while the front foot is planted on the ground

nosegrind
a move where the skater grinds across an obstacle with only the front truck

ollie
a move where the skater pops the skateboard into the air with his or her feet

pop shuvit
a move where the skater ollies and spins the board 180 degrees before landing on the board again

HOW DO YOU **LIVE**?

written by
MICHAEL A. STEELE

Michael A. Steele has been in the entertainment industry for almost twenty years. He worked in many capacities of film and television production, from props and special effects all the way up to writing and directing. For the past fifteen years, Mr. Steele has written exclusively for family entertainment. For television and video, he wrote for shows including *WISHBONE, Barney & Friends,* and *Boz, The Green Bear Next Door.* He has also authored over sixty books for various characters, including Batman, Shrek, Spider-Man, Garfield, G.I. Joe, Speed Racer, Sly Cooper, and The Penguins of Madagascar.

pencils and colors by
FERNANDO CANO

Fernando Cano is an all-around artist living in Monterrey, Mexico. He currently works as a concept artist for video game company CGbot. Having published with Marvel, DC, Pathfinder, and IDW, he spends his free time playing video games, singing, writing, and above all, drawing!

inks by
LAURA RIVERA

Laura Rivera lives in San Nicolas, Mexico. She currently works as a concept artist in the video game industry, doing what she loves most: drawing! During her free time, she enjoys building projects, photography, and playing with her dog.